SPOOK SCHOOL

REVENGE OF THE STINK-MONSTER

PETE JOHNSON

Illustrated by
Tom Percival

Stripes

Collect all the
Spook School titles:

LAIR OF THE MOTHMAN
Curse of the Rat-beast
HORROR FROM THE DEEP

Praise for Spook School:

"A fantastically humorous series from a widely admired children's author who really knows how to get readers hooked on reading." Julia Eccleshare, www.lovereading4kids.co.uk

SPOOK SCHOOL

REVENGE OF THE STINK-MONSTER

To Phoebe K. With my grateful thanks for all your interest and enthusiasm. Looking forward to your review of this one! ~ PJ

The pictures in this book are dedicated to anyone who's ever gone out of their way to be nice to someone who looks sad ~ TP

STRIPES PUBLISHING
An imprint of Magi Publications
1 The Coda Centre, 189 Munster Road,
London SW6 6AW

A paperback original
First published in Great Britain in 2010

Text copyright © Pete Johnson, 2010
Illustrations copyright © Tom Percival, 2010

ISBN: 978-1-84715-137-7
The right of Pete Johnson and Tom Percival to be identified
as the author and illustrator of this work respectively has
been asserted by them in accordance with the Copyright,
Designs and Patents Act, 1988.

A CIP catalogue record for this book is available
from the British Library.

Printed and bound in the UK.

1 2 3 4 5 6 7 8 9 10

Chapter One
Finding the Invisible Ghost

"Charlie, you're shaking."

"So are you!" I shouted back. "You're shaking and wobbling like a great big jelly." Then I added, "We've faced some terrifying monsters before – but never an invisible ghost."

Lewis and I are ghosts too, although we'd much rather be called spooks. And we're in the Spook Squad which is really cool, as it means we get to fly to

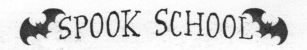

Earth to solve terrifying, ghostly mysteries.

But we've had exams all week. We've been tested on how quickly we can shape-change into snakes and make giant spiders appear out of the air. There's even been a big flying race.

Tonight was our last and toughest exam of all: tracking down an invisible ghost in just five minutes. The ghost would be hiding somewhere inside our school. And right now Lewis and I were flying around, waiting for the signal to be allowed inside.

Then we heard it: an eerie howl.

"Here we go," I said. "We'll find that invisible ghost all right because we're a great team."

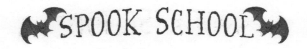

SPOOK SCHOOL

"Oh, we're the best," said Lewis, grinning at me.

Normally, our school would be full of spooks, floating up and down the long, dusty corridors as they went off to their lessons. There they would learn really important stuff, like how to fly through doors and how to shape-change. But tonight the school was deserted — except for Lewis and me.

All evening, pairs of spooks had been trying to find this invisible ghost, but so far no one had succeeded. Lewis and I were the last to try.

"The school feels so strange when it's all quiet and still," I said.

"But there's a ghost hiding in here somewhere," said Lewis. "And we've got to track it down really fast."

We stood waiting for the signal to start. And then it came: a second howl. Only this one was so loud all the cobwebs hanging from the ceiling began to shake. Our five minutes started NOW!

HOOOWL!

"Right," said Lewis. "I'll try the classrooms on the right; you check the ones on the left. Howl if you see anything. And good luck."

"We don't need luck," I cried, "because we've got talent."

I flew wildly round the classrooms. There's one big clue to finding an invisible ghost. The air where the ghost is hiding turns much, much colder. So I just had to find a patch of freezing air. That shouldn't be too hard, should it?

I flew faster and faster round the eerily quiet classrooms. Come on, where was that icy air? But try as I might, I just couldn't find it. Maybe Lewis had. I listened hard for his howl.

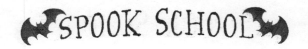
SPOOK SCHOOL

Absolutely nothing. And then suddenly
I heard it. I set off at top speed. There
was Lewis in the corridor, but instead
of looking triumphant, he seemed
totally dejected.

"I can't find the ghost anywhere,"
he said.

"Neither can I. And we're running
out of time."

"Thanks for reminding me," Lewis
snapped. Then he added, "So where
can it be? We've searched every single
room."

"There's one room we've missed,"
I said, "Spookmaster's Chamber of
Horrors." That's my nickname for
Spookmaster's study.

Spookmaster is head of Spook School.

And he's the scariest headmaster in the whole universe.

"We can't go into Spookmaster's study," said Lewis.

"I don't see why not," I replied. "We were told the ghost could be anywhere in the school." Then I added, "But I'll go on my own if you like, and then I'll be the only one to get told off."

"No, don't be stupid," said Lewis. "We'll both go."

Thick fog floated around us as we

made our way to Spookmaster's study. We both hesitated.

"In we go," said Lewis, trying to sound confident. We flew through the door. The room was like any head teacher's study — with a huge desk and a large chair. But Spookmaster rarely sat there. He was usually found sitting cross-legged up near the ceiling. Both Lewis and I immediately looked up, just to check he wasn't there tonight. Very happily, he wasn't.

I floated past Spookmaster's desk and stopped in my tracks. "Lewis," I hissed, "the air is really freezing here."

Lewis was across the room like a shot. "So it is," he said, grinning.

We'd found the ghost. Now we just had to trap it.

"Can I do the next bit?" I asked. "Please?"

"Yeah, all right," Lewis replied a bit reluctantly. "But be quick."

We'd been taught how to do this only last week. So I'd had very little practice. And I had to get it right. First, I imagined a large, white star.

14

Then I said, "Star-shape, show swiftly," which is pretty hard to say when you're as excited as I was.

In a flash, a large, white star appeared just below the ceiling. Then it dropped down to the exact spot where the ghost was hiding.

All at once, the ghost was invisible no longer. A strong, white light now lit up the familiar shape of our very own teacher: Top Ghoul. She smiled at us and said, "Well done, spooks."

Just then a tall figure appeared in the doorway. "Your exam is over!" boomed a familiar voice.

It was Spookmaster.

"Now," Spookmaster went on, soaring over our heads, his black gown flapping around him. "You had to complete this task in five minutes. And, you took…" he paused for a moment, "…four minutes and fifty-six seconds."

"Yes!" I cried.

"That means," said Spookmaster, still looking stern but not quite as stern as usual, "you have passed every

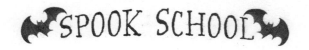

one of your exams – and you are the only students to track down an invisible ghost in five minutes."

"Just call me a genius." I grinned.

Spookmaster frowned. "Your handwriting in the written paper on the history of ghosts was atrocious, Charlie. You only just passed that one. So don't be so big-headed. But as a reward for tracking down Top Ghoul," said Spookmaster, "you will each receive a gold star."

"Oh wow," burst out Lewis.

"Double wow," I added.

"A gold star is the greatest honour you can receive at Spook School," said Top Ghoul, smiling proudly at us. "And Spookmaster only usually gives out two

or three gold stars a year."

"Come over here," said Spookmaster.
We flew towards him.

Close up, Spookmaster looked more
than ever like an extremely fierce,
incredibly ancient lion. His gaze was
fixed now on Lewis and me, and I
twisted about uncomfortably. I felt as
if he could see right inside my head
and find out all the naughty things
I'd done.

Suddenly, there was a pinging noise
and the brightest, shiniest gold star
you've ever seen popped up on the lapel
of my jacket. There was one gleaming
away on Lewis's jacket, too.

I stared down at my star proudly.
"Cool!"

"Well done," Lewis whispered.

"Well done yourself," I whispered back.

Top Ghoul congratulated us both, and then floated away. I wondered if we were supposed to float after her, but neither she nor Spookmaster spoke.

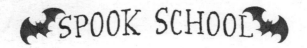

Lewis and I hovered about a little nervously for a moment, and then flew towards the door.

"Why are you leaving?" demanded Spookmaster. "I haven't finished with you yet." We stopped in our tracks and exchanged worried looks.

After giving us the gold stars, surely Spookmaster wasn't about to tell us off. What could we possibly be in trouble for now?

But then Spookmaster said, "I have another invisible ghost I want you to track down ... but on Earth this time. So, come closer and I'll fill you in."

We grinned with relief and both flew up to Spookmaster again.

"This is great news," I said.

"We'll find the ghost for you, no problem," added Lewis.

"But this will be your most baffling case yet. So listen carefully," said Spookmaster. "It concerns a couple, Jim and Daisy Renton, who recently bought a small hotel in the country. It had become rather run down, and they have worked hard to make it special. They spent weeks painting and cleaning it, but the night it opened something very strange happened. While the guests were eating, the dining room was filled with a terrible smell."

"Perhaps Jim needs to have a bath."
I giggled.

Spookmaster gave a roar of
annoyance. "When I want you to make
silly comments, Charlie, I will tell you."
I immediately stopped giggling. He
went on. "At first Jim and Daisy
thought there must be a problem with
the drains."

For some reason this made me want
to laugh again, but I just managed to
hold it in.

"They sent for the plumbers, but
they couldn't find anything wrong.
And meanwhile, this smell has got
worse. Last night it was so bad, Jim
and Daisy even had to give all the
guests masks."

SPOOK SCHOOL

I imagined all the guests slurping soup in their masks and whispered to Lewis, "Here's your menu, your bread roll and your mask." He was trying hard not to laugh as well.

Spookmaster continued. "Jim and Daisy's whole business is being ruined — and they have no idea who or what is causing the smell. But I strongly suspect it's a ghost — an invisible ghost. There are a few who hide themselves away so they can cause trouble. It could be the ghost of someone Jim and

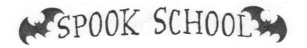

Daisy once knew. Or it might just be a very bad ghost who enjoys creating chaos. I want you to find out what's going on, and if it is a ghost, get it to stop."

"Don't worry," I said, "we'll sort out the Stink-Monster."

As soon as I said this Lewis burst out laughing. "The Stink-Monster," he repeated, grinning. "I like it."

But Spookmaster's face was one massive frown. "I'm wondering if I picked the right two members of Spook Squad for this mission. I have no time for silly spooks."

"Oh, we're not silly," I said quickly. "Honestly, we're not. We'll crack this case for you really fast, I know we will.

Actually, Spookmaster, if we solve it by midnight can we each have another gold star?" I immediately wished I hadn't said that. That's my trouble – I say stuff without thinking.

Spookmaster gave me a furious glare. I was sure he was going to tell me off again. But instead, he said, "Yes, all right."

"Great," I cried, but I felt uneasy too. Spookmaster had said, "Yes, all right" in a sly kind of way.

Then he added, "But if you don't solve the mystery by midnight, I'll take away the gold stars you've both won."

"Oh, what!" I said. I hadn't expected that at all. Lewis let out a loud gasp, and gave me an angry stare.

"Lewis, as usual, is in charge of this mission," said Spookmaster. "Be ready to leave at seven o'clock tomorrow evening. Top Ghoul will give you details of where you're going. Try and get a good day's sleep now – I think you may need it."

Outside, Lewis turned on me. "You've always got to do it, haven't you?"

SPOOK SCHOOL

"Do what?"

"Show off," shouted Lewis. "And now you might lose us our stars."

"Stop worrying, we'll solve the case."

"Will we?" said Lewis. "We're not arriving at the hotel until seven o'clock. And we've got to have it wrapped up by midnight. We've never solved a case that fast before."

"Ah, but you're forgetting one thing," I said.

"What's that?"

"I've got a supersonic brain. Can't you hear it whizzing away?"

But Lewis didn't laugh. Instead, he said, "Getting that gold star tonight meant a lot to me. And if I lose it because of you—"

"You won't," I interrupted. But even
I was a bit worried now. We flew to our
dormitory. All the spooks wanted to
see our gold stars and hear how we'd
tracked down the invisible ghost. Then
we told them about the Stink-Monster.

Just as we were finally going to
sleep, Lewis whispered to me, "You do
remember what Spookmaster said. I'm
in charge of this mission."

"Of course I do," I replied.

"Well, don't forget it," he snapped.
And I knew he was still cross with me
for showing off in front of Spookmaster.

It was late afternoon when I woke up.
Lewis was already awake. He was
studying some notes Top Ghoul had

SPOOK SCHOOL

given us about tracking down invisible
ghosts, and I could tell he was still a bit
grumpy with me. But soon it was time
to leave. All the other spooks came to
see us off, and gave us a huge good luck
howl. Top Ghoul told us the address and
then we were ready to go. We gave a
parting howl, said, "Spook-travel to
Oaktree Hotel, Buckinghamshire",
and imagined ourselves there.
Then we were off, travelling
down a massive slide which

SPOOK SCHOOL

seemed to go on for ever.

Finally we landed on Earth, at exactly seven o'clock. We could hear a radio blaring out the news.

It had been raining and the air smelt of damp earth. I sniffed appreciatively. "No bad smells here," I said.

"The stink is *inside* the hotel, you idiot," said Lewis, pointing at a grand old house in front of us. "And thanks to you, we've got just five hours to solve the whole mystery. So come on…"

Chapter Three

The Stink-Monster Strikes

Oaktree Hotel was set on the side of a big hill. Although it was getting dark, we could see that it was surrounded by beautiful countryside. Over the front door, a gleaming new sign swayed gently in the breeze. The words, "Oaktree Hotel" were painted across the top. And below that: "A warm welcome from Jim and Daisy Renton".

"So let's go inside," I said, "and get a warm welcome from Jim, Daisy and Stinky."

"OK," said Lewis, "but just remember – although no one can see us, they can *hear* us, so we must whisper at all times."

"Of course I remember," I muttered, yawning loudly. "You fuss too much."

We floated through the red-curtained windows into the hotel reception. The only smell was that of freshly-baked bread – one of the best smells ever. I bet it tasted delicious, too. That's the thing I miss most as a spook – eating. Inside the dining room a large fire blazed and crackled. It looked a cosy, comfortable room, but only three of its eight tables were occupied.

SPOOK SCHOOL

A man of about sixty, with a neatly trimmed moustache and blue twinkling eyes, was racing around serving the guests. He had to be Jim. He smiled broadly at one of the guests as he placed a steaming plate of spaghetti in front of him. The man thanked him and said, "Didn't this place used to be called 'The Avalon'?"

"That's right," said Jim, "but when Daisy and I bought it, we wanted to make it our own so we gave it a new name."

"And are you settling in here all right?" asked the guest.

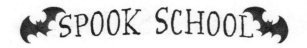

"Oh yes, we love it, although we've had a few teething problems." Jim's voice quavered as he said this.

No doubt he was remembering all the bad stinks he'd had to put up with lately. Luckily, none of the guests seemed to know anything about this. And Jim was obviously hoping they'd never have to, either.

I took a deep sniff. "Can't smell anything yet," I whispered.

"Let's search the hotel to see if we can find any freezing cold patches," said Lewis.

So Lewis flew round the guest rooms while I examined the kitchen. A friendly-looking woman with glasses all misted up with steam was bustling about preparing the dinner. This had to be Daisy. Then a boy shuffled in and picked up a tray of food for the dining room. "If anything else happens…" he began.

"I'm sure everything's going to be fine tonight, Nick," said Daisy quickly.

"I hope so," said Nick. He let out a deep sigh. "Because I can't work somewhere with such bad smells. It really upsets my nose."

Back in the dining room two more guests had arrived, a mother and daughter. The sharp-featured daughter,

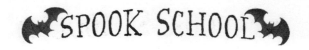

who looked about six, was glaring at
the menu, while Jim hovered nearby,
smiling anxiously. "Come on, you must
eat something, Priscilla," said her mum.

"But all this food sounds disgusting,"
said Priscilla.

"She's such a fussy eater," said her
mum proudly. Jim's smile grew more
and more fixed.

"Hey," whispered a voice down my
ear. "You're supposed to be finding an
invisible ghost not watching the guests."

"Sorry," I whispered back. "Did you
find anything?"

Lewis shook his head.

"Maybe the ghost's outside," I said.
"Or maybe it's gone somewhere else."

"So what if nothing happens

tonight?" asked Lewis.

"We'll tell Spookmaster exactly that," I replied. "He can't take our gold stars away because no ghost appeared."

"Can't he?" said Lewis gloomily.

Jim left with another order and Nick came in with a massive jug of water for Priscilla.

"Priscilla only likes certain kinds of water," said her mum.

But Nick wasn't listening. Instead he glanced around the room and sniffed loudly. "Oh no," he yelled, "my poor nose! It's here again."

"What is?" demanded Priscilla's mum.

Nick didn't answer, he just slammed the jug on the table, sloshing water everywhere and ran out of the room.

SPOOK SCHOOL

"What extraordinary behaviour," began Priscilla's mum. "I've never…" She stopped. "What on Earth *is* that?"

The smell of mouldy, very stinky socks had wafted into the room. It was soon joined by the stench of rotting fish and stale eggs. Then something even worse filled the air: the stink of fresh dog poo. And if reading that

makes you feel a bit sick, just imagine what it was like having to smell it.

It was as if twenty stink bombs had been thrown into the room all at once.

The man who'd ordered the spaghetti stopped mid-forkful, letting the strands dribble all the way down his chin. Then he let out a dramatic, "Ugh!"

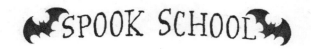

"I couldn't agree more," I whispered to Lewis. "Gross or what?"

Lewis just nodded. The smell was so ghastly he could hardly speak. Then he gasped, "The ghost who's doing this must be close by ... got to find him."

"Yeah, all right," I replied. I really didn't want to fly about in this cloud of stink. But this was our chance.

Meanwhile, all the guests had been engulfed by the smell. Some were bent double they were coughing so much. Others were dabbing their streaming eyes with hankies, while Priscilla was announcing over and over, "I'm going to be sick! I'm going to be sick!"

Jim sped in and immediately started opening the windows, but nothing

could stop this tidal wave of stink.
Then he shouted, "Don't worry, ladies
and gentlemen, help is at hand." He
went charging off and returned
moments later with skeleton masks.
"These were the only ones in our local
shop – but please put them on," he
urged the guests.

As Jim attended to the guests, Lewis and I whirled round the dining room, searching for the invisible ghost. "You must have found something," said Lewis desperately.

"Not a thing," I said. "But how is it managing to stay hidden?"

"Some ghosts are very crafty – and make sure they never stay anywhere long enough for the air to get cold," said Lewis. "But it's got to stop at some point and when it does, we'll catch it. So keep looking."

Meanwhile, Daisy was trying to persuade Priscilla and her mum to put on the skeleton masks. "No, it's horrible," said Priscilla, throwing the mask on the floor. "I'm not wearing it."

44

"But it'll help keep the smell away," said Daisy, picking it up again.

"No, I want some water first!" shouted Priscilla, while holding her nose tightly.

"Let me get you some, darling," cried her mum, picking up the jug of water.

I was floating right above Priscilla and her mum when I felt the air turn icy cold. "Gotcha," I muttered. I was so excited, but I had to act fast. There was no time to even call Lewis, who was flying round the other side of the room. So instead I pictured a star in my head. Then I started to chant, "Star-shape, show swiftly."

But I'd only got as far as "Star-shape", when a fresh blast of that grisly

stink came rushing towards me. It took
me completely by surprise. That's why
I did something really, really bad. I let
out a massive, ear-splitting
BURP!

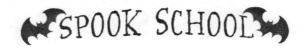

Priscilla's mum heard that all right. She jumped in shock, sending the water flying all over Priscilla. "Aaah!" she shrieked. "Not only disgusting smells, but this place is haunted as well."

Moments later, she and all the other guests stampeded out of the dining room, still coughing and choking from the smell.

Lewis flew over to me looking very angry indeed. "What did you do that for?" he hissed.

"It was an accident," I whispered. "I found the ghost. But just as I was chanting all that star-shape stuff it fired its stink right at me."

"You still shouldn't have burped like that," hissed Lewis.

"I know."

"And now you've made everything even worse. Look – all the guests are leaving."

And so they were. "I've never stayed in such a smelly hotel," cried Priscilla's mum, "and with a rude ghost yelling down my ear as well. You should be shut down."

All the other guests were shouting and coughing in agreement, as they hurried through the reception and into the cold night air.

"That stinky ghost has caused so much trouble," I said. "When I get hold of it I'll … well, it'll be very sorry."

"We've got to find Stinky first," said Lewis. "So come on."

We spent the next few hours searching every nook and cranny of that hotel. But there was no sign of the ghost. And then the clock in the hall began to strike midnight.

"Time's up," said Lewis, frowning at me. "And we've lost."

Chapter Four

Helping Jim and Daisy

We flew outside, and Lewis — as the leader of the mission — went off to speak to Spookmaster. Ghosts are at their most powerful around midnight. So Lewis just had to clear his mind and wait for Spookmaster's voice to pop into his head.

A few minutes later he flew back, looking really fed-up. "So what did Spookmaster say?" I asked.

"Oh, he said very well done," said Lewis.

"Really?" I cried.

"No, of course he didn't," snapped Lewis. "He said he hoped this would teach us not to be boastful or show off in future." Lewis was looking right at me as he said this. And then we heard two soft, pinging noises. They were our gold stars disappearing.

"That gold star never matched my jacket anyway," I joked. Lewis gave me a furious glare.

"Sorry," I said quietly.

Lewis didn't answer.

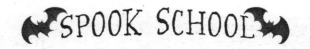

"You're supposed to say that's all right, it doesn't matter," I went on. Then I added, "I really, really am sorry. How many more times do you want me to say it?"

"One million," said Lewis.

"OK, I'll say sorry a million times, starting now."

"Don't you dare," said Lewis.

A flicker of a smile crossed his face then and he said, "I told Spookmaster we'd still like to stay on to solve this mystery, and help Jim and Daisy – and he said we could."

"Well, that's something then," I said cheerfully.

Then we noticed that Jim and Daisy were outside too, strolling in the garden.

Daisy looked as if she'd been crying. "We're ruined," she said.

Jim shook his head.

"Yes, we are," she cried. "We've poured our entire savings into this hotel. And it's all my fault. You never really wanted to come here, did you?"

"Yes, I did," Jim cried.

"No, you were never that keen," said Daisy, "and I thought you would be, as you used to live so near here as a boy." Then she added, "Did you ever hear rumours of this hotel being haunted?"

"Never," he said at once.

"And you don't think a ghost could be doing all this?" she asked.

Jim hesitated for a moment, but then said firmly, "No, because ghosts don't

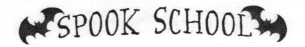

exist. I'm sure they don't."

Lewis and I grinned at each other.

The bell in reception rang. "Come on," said Jim. "One of the four guests we somehow persuaded to stay on needs us." They trudged back inside, and I suddenly felt really sorry for them.

"Why is this ghost picking on poor Jim and Daisy?" I said.

"Maybe it's an old enemy," said Lewis.

"I can't imagine them having any enemies – they're too nice," I said, racking my brains for an explanation. "I know! Maybe once there was a guy who really liked Daisy. But she married Jim instead, and now all these years later he's being really stinky about it. What do you think?"

"Rubbish," said Lewis.

"Well, you think of something then."

"I would if you'd stop talking for a moment," said Lewis. "The ghost must have a reason. If only we could find out what it is…"

I stared up at the new sign: "Oaktree Hotel".

And then suddenly an idea began to form in my head. And as it did I became very excited. In fact, I flew round and round in a mad whirl. Lewis watched me looking quite concerned.

I grinned at him. "Guess what, Lewis, I've just solved the whole mystery!"

Chapter Five

The Mystery Solved

"You've what?" spluttered Lewis.

"Yeah, listen," I cried, "this hotel has probably been haunted by a ghost for years. But it's been very quiet, as ghosts haunting places are supposed to be. But recently something has happened which has made the ghost really angry…" I paused. "Now, what's the one thing ghosts hate?"

"Change," said Lewis at once.

"Exactly. Ghosts want the place they're haunting to stay exactly the same for ever. Now, recently this hotel has had new owners."

"I'm sure it's had tons of new owners over the years…" said Lewis.

"But I bet they've always kept the same name for the hotel – until now."

Lewis looked at me. "And you think this ghost is so furious that this place isn't 'The Avalon' any more that it's making a massive stink about it?"

I nodded furiously.

He considered. "I'm not sure."

"It's a brilliant idea," I cried, swooping around him excitedly. "Go on, admit it."

"OK," said Lewis. "Just suppose

you're right. How are we going to test it out?"

"That's the problem," I agreed. "We can't exactly float up to Jim and say, 'Take that sign down and put the old one back, and your ghost will stop being stinky'."

Then Lewis had an idea. "How about if Jim thinks he's hearing it in a dream?"

"I like it," I said.

"And in the dream we'll tell him to take the sign down," went on Lewis.

"Let's do it," I said.

"Well, we've got to wait until he's asleep first," said Lewis.

We floated into reception. Daisy must have gone to bed, but Jim was sitting at the desk, and he was fast asleep.

"Poor guy, too tired to even go to bed," said Lewis. "Right, this is our chance – we've got to wake him up, but make him think he's still asleep."

Lewis flew over and blew on Jim's face, but nothing happened. "He must be really tired," I whispered.

He blew harder, but still Jim didn't

wake. Then we both blew down his ears. "Come on, Jim," I muttered. Then I yelled down his ear, "Jim, wake up!"

He heard that all right, in fact he almost jumped out of his skin. "What!" he cried. "Who's there?"

"Us," said Lewis, "Charlie and me. Only you can't see us."

"Because this is a kind of dream,"
I added.

Jim gaped. "What's going on?"

"Don't be alarmed," said Lewis. "But
we're bringing you a warning. You must
take down your 'Oaktree Hotel' sign."

"Take it down? Why?" asked Jim.

"Because…" Lewis struggled to
explain why. "Because your ghost
doesn't like it. So you've got to put up
the old sign for 'The Avalon'. Do that
and you'll never have any bad smells
again. We guarantee it."

"But who are you?" demanded Jim.
"And why can't I see you?"

"That's not important," said Lewis.
"Just get that sign down as soon as
you can."

"If what you say is true…" began Jim.

"It is," said Lewis firmly.

"…then I'm going to take that sign down right now."

"But it's nearly one o'clock in the morning," said Lewis.

"I don't care," cried Jim, leaping to his feet and rubbing his eyes. "I'm off to do it right now." He grabbed a torch and dashed outside.

We hadn't meant for him to act quite that quickly. I looked at Lewis and he shrugged. "Well, I suppose it can't do any harm," he said.

Outside there was no moon, but the sky was crammed with stars. There was a slight wind too, making the trees sway and sigh.

Jim quickly found his ladder, and positioned it under the sign.

"Wouldn't it be awful if he fell," I said, as we watched him climb to the top.

"That's what I like about you," said Lewis. "You're always so cheerful."

Jim wrenched down the new sign. "Smelly ghost, this hotel is 'Oaktree' no longer," he yelled. "And I'll find the old 'Avalon' sign – or make a new one. But it will be 'The Avalon' again, I promise. Now please leave us alone."

"There we go," I said. "Another mystery solved, thanks to me. But there's no need to congratulate me or anything. Maybe Spookmaster will give us our gold—"

"Look!" Lewis pointed.

Jim was standing on top of the ladder, sniffing loudly. Then he groaned. We quickly realized why. That disgusting smell was ripping through the air again.

Then I saw a flash of movement over by the trees. "Something's out there," I said to Lewis.

"Probably just a fox," he replied, "come to see what's going on."

But I felt uneasy.

Then the shape moved. "Look," I cried, "it's not a fox, it's a..."

Lewis and I froze in horror. For slowly rising out of the darkness came one very large, very hairy claw.

Chapter Six
The Werewolf's Claw

It was the weirdest thing I'd ever seen.

A large claw, covered in dark green fur, swinging about in the air all by itself. Jim saw it too. He stared at it in terror, his eyes bulging out of his head.

And then the claw came lunging towards him. Jim's hands were shaking so much that the torch flew out of his grasp. Then the claw dived right for his face. Jim let out a terrified yell.

"What's it doing that for?" cried Lewis. "Jim could fall off the ladder."

Jim stared up at the claw, whirling and diving round his face. "Werewolf!" he yelped.

Then he started to scramble down the ladder, which is not easy when a mad claw keeps hurling itself at your face.

"We can't just watch. We've got to help Jim," I whispered to Lewis.

"But if we fly over and start giving him advice we might scare him even more," said Lewis. I could see exactly what he meant, but I was itching to do something.

Somehow, Jim clambered down the ladder. He looked up at the claw still hovering above his head. "Werewolf," he said again, "I … I…" But he never finished his sentence.

Instead, he went hurtling off towards
the hotel. Daisy was standing in the
doorway. "Jim, I wondered where you'd
gone. Whatever are you doing out here?"

"Saw … werewolf," began Jim, his
teeth chattering with fear.

Daisy put her arm round him.
"Come on, love, you've just had a
nightmare, that's all … I told you not
to have that cheese tonight." She
helped him inside and closed the door.

Lewis and I flew out from where
we'd been watching and faced the mad
claw. I know I should have waited for
Lewis to talk to it, as he was the leader,
but I was so angry. What was that
ghost playing at, terrorizing Jim
like that?

"You needn't think we're scared of you," I yelled, as it whirled around us. "I could make a claw appear too if I wanted, but I'm too cool. And what do you think you're doing? You should never use your power to bully humans. You're the stupidest, smelliest, most pathetic ghost I've ever met."

"OK, Charlie," whispered Lewis. He could tell I was really mad. "I'll take over now." He glared at the claw, still circling furiously round us like a mad wasp, and said, "Look, ghost, we don't know why you're behaving like this, and ruining Jim and Daisy's hotel. We thought it might be because you didn't like the hotel's new name. But actually, I don't care what your reason is now…"

"That's right, you tell it," I said.

"I'm ordering you, on behalf of the Spook Squad, to leave this hotel tonight – and never return. Is that clear?"

"See you, Stinky," I added. The claw had stopped moving. It just hovered there in the air. The next moment it vanished into the shadows.

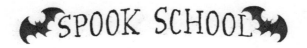

"We've done it!" I cried. "It's gone."

But Lewis wasn't convinced. "It left too easily."

"No, it could see we meant business. I mean, no one messes with the Spook Squad, we're…" But the words died on my lips.

For suddenly, out of the air, came not one but two massive furry claws. Behind them came two more … and more behind them. Wherever we looked the air was full of claws: a great seething swarm of them, all whizzing round madly, and making straight for Lewis and me.

I'd like to tell you that Lewis and I faced up to this great army of claws with amazing bravery.

SPOOK SCHOOL

I'd like to tell you that.

But actually, we were so petrified
we fled into the hotel as fast as
we could.

Chapter Seven
Help from an Ogre

"We're a disgrace," said Lewis.

"No, it's just that swarm of claws took us by surprise," I said.

"We were scared out of our wits. We ran away from the enemy," said Lewis gravely.

"Well, we're here now, checking the claws have gone," I said. "And thankfully, it looks like they have."

Lewis and I were outside Jim and

Daisy's hotel again, perched on top of
the chimney. Suddenly something came
whooshing out of the sky: something
truly gruesome. And it was heading
straight for us.

It was a ghost with one huge eye
right in the middle of its face.
Underneath that was a shrunken
nose and a gigantic mouth,
with vile yellow
teeth. There were
blotches and
pockmarks all
over its face, too.
But worst of all was
the thing hanging off the
end of its nose: a huge, grey boil.
It had another, equally massive boil

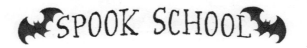

hanging down from its chin, too.

But as soon as we saw it Lewis and I were on our feet cheering. For this revolting-looking ghost was also our great friend, Oswald the ogre, who'd helped us solve the mystery of the rat-beast.

"Ain't this a surprise?" cried Oswald, landing beside us.

When spooks are happy they soar right up into the air. And that's what Lewis, Oswald and I did just then, spinning round and round each other.

"But what are you doing here?" I asked, as we settled back on the roof. Oswald haunted miles away in Marlow.

"Your really scary boss—" began Oswald.

SPOOK SCHOOL

"Spookmaster," I interrupted.
"That's the geezer. He asked me to
fly in and give you both a bit of help."

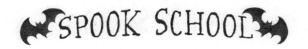

Normally I'd have felt cross about this, but I was so pleased to see Oswald I quickly swallowed down any annoyance. And anyway, Lewis and I did need some help.

"Come on now, tell me everything," said Oswald. So we did.

"It's the worst ghost we've ever tackled," I said, "and the most confusing. I mean, at first it just left behind a bad stink."

"But a stink so vile it made the guests feel so sick they had to leave Jim and Daisy's hotel," cut in Lewis. "So then we thought that the ghost was cross because they've changed the name of the hotel. And we got Jim to take down the new sign—"

"Only that just seemed to get the ghost even madder," I interrupted, "and it attacked Jim with a huge furry claw. I mean, what's all that about?"

"I need to think about this," said Oswald. "Excuse me, mateys." He floated up into the air, and stayed there grunting and muttering for a few seconds.

Then he flew down towards us again, his bright yellow teeth grinning away. "You know what I think? For some reason this ghost doesn't like Jim. And it wants him out of this hotel."

"Well, we guessed that," I said, "but why?"

"Easy to find out," said Oswald. "Let's ask it."

"Oh yeah…" I began, "we can't even get it to show itself."

"I'll get it to appear," cried Oswald, his eyes gleaming with mischief, "by shape-changing into Jim. Then I'll start shouting very rude stuff about a smelly ghost. I'm sure the ghost'll pop up then. And when it does I'll change back to my normal good-looking self." He started to chuckle. "And we'll all have a good natter, and you two spooks can tell it to behave itself."

Before we could say anything more Oswald was swooping off to take a peek at Jim. "Because," he explained, "I can't shape-change into someone if I don't know what they look like. Don't worry," he added, "I'll tiptoe."

Hard to imagine Oswald ever tiptoeing, but he was back in a flash. "Jim's sleeping like a baby, and while he's asleep we're going to sort out all his problems for him. Now, you two whippersnappers keep out of the way, but as soon as Stinky pops up…"

"We'll fly over," I said. "You know, I think your plan might just work."

"Of course it will! Leave everything to Oswald," he said.

Moments later, he had turned into Jim. Then he started shouting, "Come on, ghost, show yourself. You don't scare me. All you can do is smell and then smell some more."

"Oswald's really enjoying himself," whispered Lewis, as we watched from the roof. "I just hope his plan works."

"Hey, Mr Angry Pants!" yelled "Jim". "Where are you?"

At that moment two huge hairy claws tore out of the darkness and instantly knitted on to arms. Then a face covered with wolf hair pushed its way into the darkness, its red eyes blazing with rage. Suddenly, its jaws snapped together, and it leaped forward at "Jim", howling with fury.

SPOOK SCHOOL

"Jim" gave a yelp of horror, yelled,
"Run lads!" and flew off at an incredible
speed into the hotel. Lewis and I were
right behind him.

Chapter Eight

Battling the Claws

"Nothing frightens me," said Oswald,
"except werewolves. There's just
something about them. Still, I feel I've
let you two down."

"No, you haven't," I said. "Anyway,
we ran away from it too."

"Twice in one night," added Lewis.

It was the following evening.
Oswald had slept over, but now he had
to return home, because of Mrs Pearce

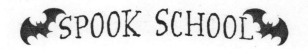

(that's the human whose house he haunts). "She worries if I'm away too long," said Oswald. "But you know what you've got to do tonight."

I nodded. We'd chatted about it with Oswald as soon as we woke up. "We'll get this stinky werewolf mad again," I said, "only this time we definitely won't run away from it – no matter what it does. And we'll make sure it leaves this hotel for good tonight."

"That's the *spirit*, lads," said Oswald, and we all grinned at his little joke. "I wish I could stay and fight alongside you," he said. "I might have conquered my fear of werewolves."

"It's not a problem," said Lewis, "and you've been a brilliant help to us."

"You really have," I agreed.

Oswald's boils glowed with pride. "Well, that's what I like doing more than anything else: helping my mates." And then he took off into the air. "One last tip," he called, "there's one thing all werewolves fear — silver bullets. Never forget that." Then he was gone.

Lewis and I flew into the hotel. "Right," said Lewis, looking at me. "No more running away, no matter how frightening this werewolf looks."

"Agreed," I yelled. Then I clamped my hand over my mouth. Daisy had been walking past us with a tray of soup and prawn cocktails, and nearly dropped it with shock. Still looking anxious, she sped into the dining room.

"Oops, sorry, I forgot they can hear us," I said.

"Just try not to say anything," said Lewis, "and we won't get the werewolf mad until after the hotel closes for the night. We don't want to scare off any other guests."

Daisy made a big fuss over the one family who were left, promising them "good, wholesome home cooking". She was doing most of the work. There was no sign of Nick, and Jim was walking about in a dream – not surprising really, after what had happened to him last night.

Then, just as Jim was bringing in the main course a great whirling cloud of stink rose up again.

"The Stink-monster has landed,"
I whispered to Lewis.

And the smell was even more
disgusting tonight. Jim stood there
holding his nose and muttering, "Oh
no, it's here again."

Daisy rushed in with the skeleton masks, but the mother of the family shook her head. "We like your hotel. But we really can't sit here and eat, while wearing these silly masks. I'm sorry but we're going to have to leave too."

After the family had gone, we watched Daisy switch off all the lights in the dining room, holding a handkerchief up to her nose as she did so. She turned to her husband. "You know, Jim," she said, "there's no natural reason for what's happening. I'm beginning to wonder if this hotel just doesn't want us here. I even thought I heard a ghost shouting at me tonight."

Lewis shook his head at me.

"We'll just have to sell up," said Daisy, "and try and get some of our money back. But first I think we need a good night's sleep. Come on." They both trudged upstairs.

"Right," said Lewis. "It's time to get to work. I reckon the werewolf is still hiding in the dining room because it stinks in there. We've got to make it appear again, so will you get it angry?"

"With pleasure," I said.

I floated into the dining room. The air was heavy and stale and pongy, and the stench seemed to reach out to meet me.

"Hey, Stink-werewolf," I shouted. "I'm telling you to stop blowing off and leave this hotel tonight – if not sooner."

I looked about eagerly for any sign of a claw: nothing.

"Come on, you big blast of stink!" I yelled.

Still nothing.

Then I added, "And stop frightening Jim. He's done nothing wrong."

All at once, something stirred in the darkest corner of the room. For some reason the ghost really didn't like poor old Jim. So I said some more stuff about him. "Jim and Daisy are such a decent couple, and you've no right to invade their hotel."

Suddenly, a werewolf's claw sprang out of the darkness. I ducked as the claw dived straight at me. And then a second shot out of the air, followed

by a third, then a fourth.

Soon the room was full of claws all hurtling like arrows towards their target: me.

I tell you, when a pack of ghost claws all pile towards you at once, it's a bit like being hit by a giant blast of air. They sent me tumbling to the floor, but I was soon up on my feet again.

Immediately the claws were back. I received another massive slap of air, and I fell to the floor a second time. Out of the corner of my eye, I saw Lewis fly into the room. But I didn't call out for help. I knew Lewis was tracking the ghost and searching for an icy patch of air. The ghost couldn't be far away – not with all these claws charging about.

I flew up again only to be surrounded by still more claws. I couldn't even count how many of them there were now. Then Lewis gave a little cry of triumph and yelled out, "Star-shape, show swiftly."

Instantly a star landed right in the far corner of the dining room.

SPOOK SCHOOL

Then it flew to exactly where the ghost
was hiding.

All the claws instantly vanished,
and I breathed a small sigh of relief.
I watched and waited as the star lit up
the corner of the room. It had such a
dazzlingly bright light, that no ghost
could hide from it.

Not even the Stink-monster.

And moments later the menacing werewolf appeared in front of us once more. Its sunken, red eyes gleamed furiously. And its huge tongue lolled out of its mouth as it let out a blood-curdling roar.

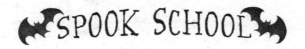

"Now look here…" Lewis managed to choke out.

"You've got to stop this," I whispered.

"Or we'll…" began Lewis. "Look, let's talk about this."

But there was no time for any more chatting – the werewolf gave another roar and lunged at Lewis. He darted out of the way just in time.

"Hey, stop that," I cried. "That's the trouble with werewolves – they have no manners. Well, come on, try and knock me to the ground again!" I was so angry with this werewolf all my fear was starting to melt away.

The werewolf swung a massive claw in my direction. "Is that the best you can do?" I taunted.

It gave another roar and dived straight at me. "Look out," yelled Lewis.

"I'm fine," I cried. And amazingly, I really was. "So you want to play, do you, Werewolf? Come on, show me what you can do."

Enraged now, the werewolf leaped at me. But to my huge surprise it stopped in mid-air, and just hung there. But why? What had happened?

I looked at Lewis.

"I didn't do anything…" he said.

Then we realized why it had stopped. Someone had heard us shouting, and was coming downstairs. The dining room door creaked open.

We had company.

Chapter Nine
Fighting a Werewolf

It was Jim, and it was clear right away
that he could see the werewolf. He
pointed at it, speechless with fear.

All at once the werewolf came to life
again: shaking its head and baring its
massive teeth, snarling and snapping.
Then it charged towards him.

Jim looked as if he was about to faint.
He backed away from it, throwing his
hands up to his face to protect himself

from its razor-sharp claws. The werewolf couldn't actually do anything to Jim, but right now he didn't realize that. We had to help Jim — and fast.

It was then that I remembered the last thing Oswald had told us: silver bullets were the one thing which stopped werewolves. But would it work on a ghost werewolf too? And could I magic one up? Quick as a flash I closed my eyes and said, "Silver bullet, strike the werewolf!"

The werewolf was lunging right at Jim's throat now, its teeth bared and its huge furry claws ready to rip Jim's head off. Or that's exactly what it looked like. No wonder Jim was trembling and shaking.

And then, out of the air my silver
bullet appeared. It hovered for a
moment before flying off towards the
werewolf.

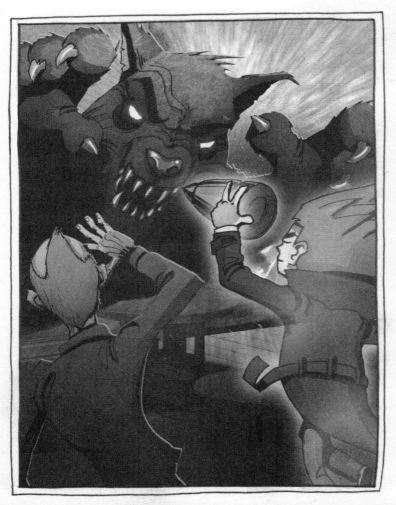

"Hey," cried Lewis. Then he looked at me. "Did you do that?"

I nodded.

I thought Lewis might be cross that I'd fired it without consulting him, but instead he said, "Top idea."

The next moment, the bullet hit the werewolf, catching it right in the throat. The creature lurched forward, saliva gushing out of its mouth. Then it let out a mighty roar of shock before it rolled on to the ground. Soon all I could see were its red eyes burning with rage, before it vanished into the darkness. But even after the werewolf had gone, Jim didn't move. He was too scared, I suppose.

"We'd better let Jim see us," said

Lewis, whispering so Jim couldn't hear
him, "and try and sort this out. After
what he's seen tonight, two more
ghosts can't be that frightening."

So that's what we did. We each closed
our eyes and said, "See me, Jim" twice.

Moments later Jim could indeed
see us.

"Now don't be alarmed," began Lewis,
"but first I think you should sit down."

"Yes, yes," croaked Jim, as he
staggered on to a chair. He still looked
as if he was in a trance.

"We're two very friendly ghosts…"
I began.

Lewis frowned at me in a "I'm doing
the talking, not you" sort of way. Then
he went on, "We've come to help you

103

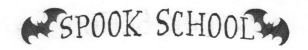

sort out this ghost who's been causing your hotel such problems."

Jim suddenly looked up at us. "That silver bullet, did you just fire it?"

"I did actually," I began proudly. "I get these good ideas…" But then I fell silent as I saw Jim frowning at me.

"Well, you shouldn't have done that," he said.

"I shouldn't?" I replied, puzzled – and a bit hurt. "Why not? Do you like being attacked by a rampaging werewolf?"

Jim ignored me. "Yesterday I knew for certain Werewolf was behind this."

I looked at him. He hadn't said "a werewolf" or "the werewolf" just "Werewolf", as if… And then an idea popped into my head and I practically yelled, "Werewolf – that's a nickname, isn't it?"

"Yes, of course it is," said Jim.

"Of a friend?" I asked.

Jim looked up. "Of my best friend."

Chapter Ten

Jim's Incredible News

"But why was your best friend called
Werewolf?" asked Lewis.

Jim smiled. "Because the poor guy
had the hairiest hands you've ever seen.
We only called him Werewolf for a
joke, but the name stuck and I don't
think he minded. His real name was
Edward. Only no one ever called him
that. Anyway, he and I both got our
first job working right here, when we

were … not much older than you two."

"Here at this hotel!" Lewis and I cried together.

"That's right," said Jim, smiling at the memory. "We worked here every weekend. We started off just doing odd jobs, cleaning and working at the tables, but gradually we were given more important things to do. And then in the summer there came the chance to work here every single day – be a proper member of staff." Jim sighed.

"But there was only one job available. And the hotel couldn't choose between Werewolf and me. We were both such good workers. So in the end they set us a competition. We each had to clean and tidy one of the hotel guest rooms. The

person whose room was judged the cleanest would get the job. We both wanted to win so badly and we worked really hard." He paused.

"So who won?" asked Lewis.

Jim didn't answer for a moment, and then he muttered very quietly, "I did."

"Well done," I said.

Suddenly a grisly snarl rang round the room. "Werewolf's back," whispered Lewis.

"Yeah, behave yourself, Werewolf," I shouted. "And stop being a bad loser."

"No, no," said Jim, "he's right to be angry. Don't worry, Werewolf, I'll tell them the rest."

The snarling immediately stopped.

Jim's head lowered and he went on

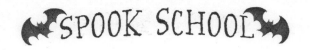

in a voice scarcely above a whisper.
"Just before the judging, I sneaked in
and took a look at the room Werewolf
had cleaned and tidied. I'd done a good
job, but he'd done a better one. His
whole room gleamed. I knew he'd win.
So I…" Jim hesitated.

"Yes," I prompted.

Jim let out the deepest sigh I'd ever
heard, and then whispered, "I walked
around the room and dropped a sweet
wrapper here, a piece of paper there."

Lewis and I gaped at him.

"You cheated," I blurted out.

Jim nodded and hung his head.
"That day, all I could think about was
winning. And, of course, after
sabotaging Werewolf's room I won the

job easily. But Werewolf quickly worked out what I'd done. He told me to own up, but I refused and took the job."

"And was that the end of your friendship?" asked Lewis.

"Oh yes," said Jim sadly. "Werewolf had really trusted me. He couldn't believe how I'd let him down. I'd lost my best friend and it was all my fault. Later, he moved away. Then many years went by until Daisy saw this very same hotel for sale. She didn't know I'd worked here, of course. And the bad thing I'd done to my best mate had happened such a long time ago, I thought I could forget it. But the very first day we arrived, a cold shiver ran down my spine." He paused. "It is

Werewolf haunting me, isn't it?"

But before Lewis or I could reply, a voice called from the darkness, "Yes, of course it is."

And then, out of the air formed the shape of a boy. A serious-looking boy with extremely hairy hands.

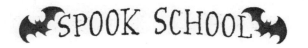

"It's Werewolf," cried Jim, "and you're just as I remember you."

"Ghosts can be any age they want," Lewis explained.

"And you found me here, Werewolf," croaked Jim.

Werewolf shook his head firmly. "Oh no, I didn't find you, you called me here."

"I did?" said Jim, looking puzzled.

"You kept thinking about me and remembering what you'd done." Werewolf's voice grew louder. "You thought about me so much that I found myself being pulled here. And the guilt poured off you like a bad smell." He was scowling at Jim now, his face all twisted up with anger. "So I just thought I'd add some smells of my own."

"And they were brilliant," I said. "The stinkiest smells I've ever sniffed."

"And then," went on Werewolf, "I decided to ruin your hotel, to make it so horrible and smelly that no one would ever want to stay here. I wanted to pay you back for what you did to me all those years ago."

"Well, you've done that all right," said Jim. "Daisy and I are going to have to sell up."

Werewolf ignored this and went on, "I wanted you to know it was me who was sabotaging your hotel. So last night, when you were messing about with the hotel sign — and what a stupid idea that was..." he said, looking at me.

"What a cheek," I muttered.

"...I decided it was time to show myself. I thought one werewolf claw would be enough."

"Yes, I guessed it was you then," said Jim. "And I can't blame you for taking revenge on me."

Jim seemed as if he was about to say something else, but stopped himself. Instead, he and Werewolf just looked at each other for a long time.

Then Lewis stepped between them. "And now you both have to listen to me," he said.

Chapter Eleven

A Final Surprise

Lewis's voice had become strong and determined. "You two were friends once, best friends. Then you did a very bad thing, Jim. But Werewolf, you've been up to some pretty nasty tricks lately, too. So now it's time for you both to say sorry and call a truce."

At first neither Jim nor Werewolf said a word, they just went on staring at each other.

"Well, come on," I cried impatiently.

Jim moved forward and said, "To deliberately ruin your best mate's chances, how nasty is that? This is something I should have said to you all those years ago. Werewolf, I'm very sorry for what I did … and very ashamed." He hung his head and went on staring at the ground until Werewolf flew right up to him and said quietly:

"You let me down so badly I felt I couldn't trust anyone else. It was a long time before I made friends again. But these past few days I've been so eaten up with revenge, I just couldn't stop. Instead, I turned into a monster. I'm very, very sorry." He stretched out a hairy hand.

Immediately, Jim tried to hold it. Of course, he couldn't as Werewolf's hand was made of air. But he still held on to the air for several seconds. And there were tears in the corners of his eyes.

Suddenly the stairs creaked. "That'll be Daisy, come to look for me," muttered Jim.

"It's time to go, Werewolf," said Lewis quickly.

Werewolf nodded. "At last you and I are friends again, Jim. Took us long enough, didn't it?"

He and Jim both laughed softly.

As Werewolf started to fade away into the shadows, he called out, "And, Jim, I'm glad you're back at our hotel. I really am."

Before Jim could reply Werewolf had vanished.

"Best friend I ever had," murmured Jim, lost in memories for a moment.

"We're going to disappear too,"

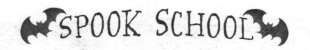

said Lewis. "But, Jim, this has all been a big shock for you, so maybe you should sit down for a bit."

Jim nodded. He shuffled over to a chair, while we made ourselves invisible again. Moments later he was fast asleep.

Then Daisy rushed in. "Jim … Jim … oh, there you are. I've been looking everywhere for you. What are you doing down here?"

Jim rubbed his eyes. "Must have fallen asleep, love," he said, blinking up at her. "I've had such a strange dream – but a good one…"

"Well, I've decided," said Daisy, "we're definitely packing up and leaving this hotel tomorrow."

Jim stood up. "Oh no, there's no need to do that," he said, smiling.

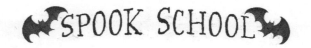

Daisy stared at him, astonished. "Why ever not?"

"Because I just know everything's going to be all right now. I really do. I've never told you this before, but I used to work at this hotel."

"You did?" cried Daisy.

"I'd like to tell you all about it," he went on, as the two of them headed upstairs.

I turned to Lewis. "Result, I think."

"Yeah, I think that's the end of the Stink-monster," said Lewis. "Let's go and tell Spookmaster."

Of course, it was just Lewis who actually talked to Spookmaster, while I waited around impatiently. When Lewis flew back to me he looked

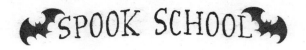

very serious. "You won't believe what's happened now."

"What?" I groaned.

And at that moment there was a soft pinging sound, as gold stars sprang up on Lewis's and my jacket.

Then I looked up at Lewis's grinning face. "You really had me going there – but how...?"

"Spookmaster was so impressed with the way we solved this mystery he said we could have our gold stars back. And he said we can stay a bit longer, just to check Jim and Daisy are all right."

"Excellent," I said. Then I added, "I've been thinking about Jim wanting to beat his best mate so badly he'd cheat."

"We'd never do that," said Lewis firmly.

"No," I agreed, "because your best mates – well, they're special."

"Talking of mates," said Lewis, "guess who's dropped in – and is waiting for us up on the roof?"

"Not Oswald!" I cried excitedly.

Lewis nodded. "He's really keen to hear how we got on."

"Well, what are we waiting for?" I replied. "Let's go and tell him the good news – and start celebrating!"

Jokes
(FOR WOLFISH FOLK)
Where do you keep your pet werewolf?
In a were-house!

Find out more about Pete Johnson at:

www.petejohnsonauthor.com